"Good catch, Ship!"

Julie Yamamoto clapped as her pet jumped up and caught a Frisbee in his mouth.

Ben Tennyson shook his head. "It's hard to believe that Ship isn't from this planet," he said. "He's like a dog in so many ways."

"He's better than a dog," Julie replied. "No fleas!"

Kevin Levin pulled into the driveway in his bright green sports car.

"It's about time," said Ben's cousin, Gwen. "The movie's going to start soon."

Kevin climbed out of the car. "So we'll miss some lousy previews," he said. "I've got something much better to show you. Check this out."

Kevin held up a round metal device. "I got it at an underground alien tech swap. Isn't it awesome?"

"What is it?" Ben asked.

Kevin shrugged. "I don't know yet. I—hey!"

Before Kevin could finish, Ship jumped up and grabbed the device right out of his hand.

"Get back here, you crazy nano-mutt!" Kevin yelled. He chased Ship across the yard.

Julie held up the Frisbee. "Here, Ship!" she called out. "Let's trade!"

Ship ran toward Julie. Kevin dove after him, reaching out to grab the device.

Zap! The device accidentally went off. A green light shot out and hit Julie.

Julie's body glowed with green light. When the light faded, Julie looked . . . different. Her body was covered with green scales. Her hands looked like claws. Ben, Gwen, and Kevin gasped.

"What's the matter?" Julie asked.

Gwen handed Julie a small mirror. "You'd better see for yourself."

"Okay, I'm lizard girl," Julie said, trying to stay cool. "There's got to be a reverse button, right?"

Kevin looked over the machine. "That would be a negative."

"I think I know what happened," said Kevin. "There was another device like this one at the swap. I bet that one is the reverse ray."

"So who got it?" Ben asked.

"The Forever Knights," Kevin replied. "No problem. We just break into their castle and steal it from them."

Ben groaned. The Forever Knights were a bunch of guys descended from the knights of old. Ben and his friends were on top of their enemies list.

"Stealing isn't the way to go," Ben said.

"What else can we do? Knock on the door and say 'pretty please'?" Kevin asked.

"All right," Ben said. "I'll go with Kevin."

"I'll hang with Julie," Gwen offered.

Ship jumped up and down.

"No way, Ship," Ben said. "I know you want to help. But you can't. The knights captured you once already."

Ben and Kevin drove through the woods to the Forever Knights' castle.

"I heard they beefed up security since the last time we were here," Kevin warned. "Breaking in could be tough."

"So what's the plan?" Ben asked. "Ring the bell and ask for a tour?"

"There's a small service door in the back," Kevin said. "It's usually not guarded."

They found the door—but it was locked shut.

"No problem," Ben said. He dialed up the Omnitrix and transformed into Goop. Then he slipped under the door and unlocked it.

"See how easy that was?" Kevin said. They stepped into a dark passageway.

Without warning, the floor opened up underneath their feet. It was a trap!

"Whoaaaaaaaaaaaa!" Ben and Kevin landed with a splash in a moat filled with black water.

Kevin felt something on his arm. He looked down to see a slimy tentacle. "Uh, Ben, I don't think we're alone."

A dozen tentacles splashed out of the water. Three of them wrapped around Kevin and started to drag him under.

Ben slapped the Omnitrix again. He transformed into another alien form—Big Chill. The blue, buglike alien grabbed Kevin and flew out of the water.

"Say freeze!" Big Chill hissed. He shot a blast of icy air at the moat. The water froze, trapping the tentacles in the ice.

"Let's keep moving," Kevin said.

They came to a door that led to another passageway. Kevin carefully took a step inside.

"No trapdoor," Kevin said. He put his other foot inside the passage . . .

. . . and triggered another booby trap. Sharp wood spears shot out of the wall.

"I got this one," Kevin said. He touched the stone wall. A moment later, his whole body had turned to stone.

Kevin charged through the passage, smashing the spears into splinters. Big Chill followed safely behind him until they reached the other side.

While Ben and Kevin made their way deeper into the castle, Julie was becoming more and more like a reptile. She pounced on a juicy moth.

"Maybe you should rethink that snack choice," Gwen advised. "I hear it's not easy to get rid of bug breath."

Kevin and Big Chill finally found their way to the weapons stash. The door was flanked by two stone gargoyle statues.

"Do you think the door is booby-trapped?" Big Chill asked.

"Could be," Kevin said. "I say we bust it down, grab the device, and get out of here."

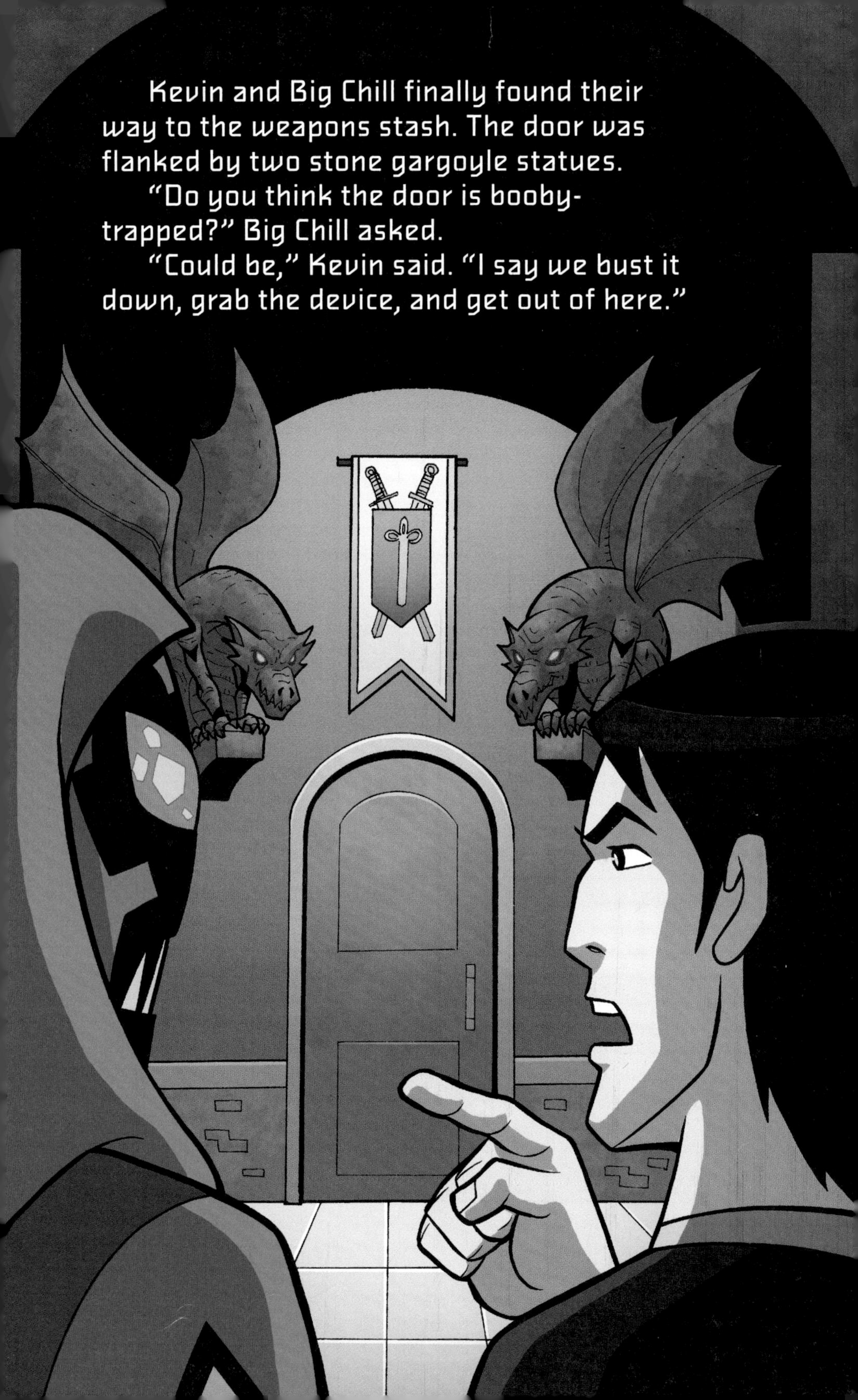

Kevin raced toward the door, ready to knock it down.

Suddenly, the eyes of the gargoyles began to glow bright red. The stone creatures came to life. They pounced on Kevin.

"Of course," Big Chill said. "They're robots!"

Kevin somersaulted between the two gargoyles, dodging them. They turned on him, shooting red laser blasts from their eyes.

Bill Chill flew down the corridor and aimed a blast of freezing breath at the gargoyles.

The frozen robots shattered into pieces.

Big Chill quickly transformed back into Ben. He opened the door to the weapons room.

"Let's make this fast," Ben said.

The room was loaded with alien tech. Kevin gave a low whistle. "Wow. What a stash."

"We're grabbing that lizard-reversing thing and getting out of here," Ben said. "No souvenirs, okay?"

"You are no fun sometimes," Kevin complained.

Kevin spotted the device on a shelf.
"Here it is," he said.
As soon as he grabbed the device, a piercing alarm echoed through the castle.

"Run!" Ben cried.

They dashed back through the castle as fast as they could. Knights poured out of every doorway, chasing them.

Ben and Kevin raced outside, and a knight tackled Kevin. As he fell, Kevin tossed the device to Ben. But a knight knocked Ben out of the way.

At that moment, Ship appeared out of nowhere! He leaped up and caught the device in his mouth.

Ben ran to the car. Behind him, Kevin had absorbed the knights' armor. Metal Kevin plowed through the knights, knocking them down. Then he jumped into the driver's seat.

"Thank goodness we got away," Ben sighed as they sped away. "What a *knight*-mare!"

The device worked perfectly. Soon Julie was back to normal.

"Thanks, guys," Julie said. "You know, I could really go for a bug—I mean, a burger."

Ben and Kevin gave Gwen a puzzled look.

Gwen just laughed. "You don't want to know!"